Maggie and the King

Story by Katy Pistole
Illustrations by Arielle Fischer

Dear Yolanda,
I love you so much!
♥ Katy

Printed in the United States of America

First Printing, 2014

ISBN 978-1500715830

Theotrope Publishing
PO Box 181
Bumpass, VA 23024

All Maggie ever wanted to do was dance.

But she always seemed to be in the way.

She found a friend to dance with...

...but sometimes, the friend would step on Maggie's toes. And that hurt.

When Maggie got older, another friend introduced her to the King.

The King could dance like nobody Maggie had ever seen. He invited Maggie to dance with Him. And she did.

Maggie and the King danced and danced.

But after a while, Maggie felt like she was in the way...

...so she began looking
for someone else
to dance with.

Maggie would find a new friend, and they might even dance, but after a while, they all stepped on her toes.

When Maggie's toes hurt too much, she would go back and dance with the King.

And in a little while, when she felt better, she would leave the King...

...and search for others to dance with.

Finally, after Maggie's toes had been squashed so often that she feared she could never dance again...

...she went back
to the King.

And she was mad.

And the King knelt and washed
her smashed toes.

"Maggie," He said, and His eyes brimmed with love. "Don't you know? You were made to dance with Me."

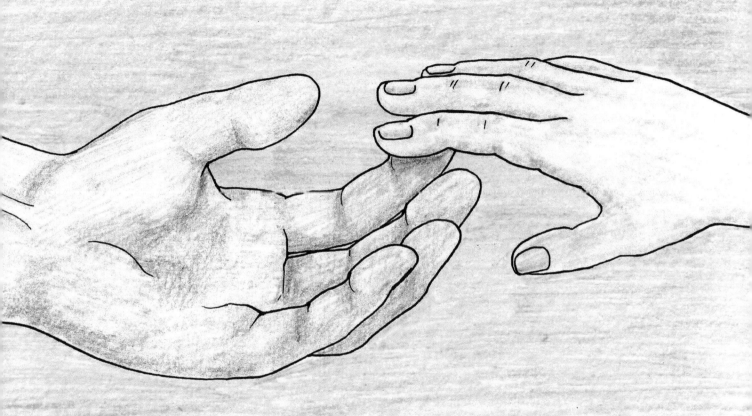

The King reached out His hand,
and she placed her tiny hand in His.

He reached out His feet, and Maggie placed her tender toes on His.

The King took Maggie in His arms and they danced and danced.

And nobody
ever stepped
on Maggie's toes
again.

About the Author

Katy Pistole is a beloved daughter of the King who loves to write about His Story and the way He invites His children to dance. Katy is also the author of the Sonrise Farm books, a horse series for youth. You can find out more about Katy at www.KatyPistole.com

About the Illustrator

Arielle Fischer has always loved drawing, especially with a simple, expressive style. She often draws animal portraits in colored pencil. Arielle also writes fiction for young adults.